THE GIRL
WHO SAVED YESTERDAY

BY
JULIUS LESTER

ILLUSTRATED BY
CARL ANGEL

When the people of the village sent the girl into the forest, it was the trees as ancient as breath who took her in and raised her. She loved living with them, but now they were asking her to leave.

"We need you to return to your village and save Yesterday," Wonderboom, the most ancient of the ancient trees, told her.

"All the Yesterdays," added Gloomy Night, whose limbs were as thick as sorrow.

Trees do not speak with words, of course, but like winds whispering to clouds. Silence, for that is what the trees had named her, did not understand what she was supposed to do.

"How do I save Yesterday?" she wanted to know.

There was a loud clattering of limbs and branches as the trees shook themselves from side to side. They didn't know, either. But Silence had learned that trees remember everything, and that they always tell the truth.

That evening as she said goodbye, she could feel that they wanted her to stay as much as she did. Some were even weeping. ThunderSnow, who had been her teacher and special friend, lifted her tenderly into his soft, broad-leafed branches. He sang her the lullaby trees soothe their children with during storms when winds and rains lash them like undeserved anger.

When Silence had fallen asleep, ThunderSnow moved quietly through the night until he came to the forest just outside the village that had sent her away. He lay her gently on the soft, yellow pine needles at the foot of a tree that had been made ill by Yesterday. Thunder-Snow hoped Silence could find the way to save this tree and all the other trees Yesterday had sickened.

It was late afternoon when Silence
awoke. She looked around and saw the road
that led to the village. She did not want to
go back there. But she knew she must.

When she reached the center of the village,
her eyes immediately saw the mountain which
loomed like a memory no one could recall. She
had been a baby when she was found at its base,
with no one to call mother or father. She was
certain they lived at the top of the mountain,
and every day she had tried to climb up there.

The villagers told her she would anger the mountain if she did, and it would send down fire and destroy everything and everyone. When she refused to obey them, the villagers felt they had no choice but to take her deep inside a distant forest and leave her there. The ancient trees there had heard her frightened heart and adopted her, but now they had sent her back.

The villagers came out of their homes and stared at the girl. Her dark skin shone as bright as the blackness which surrounds the stars and makes them gleam. She was taller now and stood as still and proud as a tree, but they knew who she was. Why had she come back?

Before anyone could ask, Sun began sliding from the sky like disappointment that would never be redeemed. Afraid, people hurried to hide in their homes, but no one thought to warn Silence that she would die if she stayed outside on this particular night.

Quickly, Darkness so thick settled on the land that Lion stuffed his roar back into his chest and ran to hide in a cave. Elephant raised her trunk and opened her mouth to trumpet a call, but then rumbled away, while Monkey scampered to the top of the highest tree and covered her eyes with her hands.

A stillness as deep and mysterious as the space between the beats of a heart came down from the mountain. Fear quivered inside Silence like leaves being pelted by a hard rain. Suddenly a redness rose from the mountain and swelled until it filled the sky.

Then it burst and split into long
narrow shafts that streaked down
like a hundred arrows shot from a
hundred bows, all shrieking like
bolts of lightning sharpened by
hopelessness, and the very land
shook as if it were sobbing.

Silence wanted to run from the arrows of light coming at her, but to her surprise, she felt only a wind as thin as a raindrop as they passed around and through her and into the village. The houses trembled like eyelashes struggling to hold back tears, while the piercing screams and sobs grew louder. She recognized those sounds. They were the same ones her heart had made when the villagers had sent her away. They were the sounds of a heart that was not loved.

Finally the time came for Morning Star to awaken Sun. The lights rose into the air and hovered over the village in a tattered sheet of dimness. Then they drifted upward as reluctantly as the last flower of summer drops its petals. Silence knew now why the trees had sent her back and what she had to do to save Yesterday.

When the people of the village slowly came outside, they were surprised to see that she was still alive.

"I need a scythe," she said before any of them spoke.

After a moment, the Iron Maker went to his shop and gave her one.

With a wide and smooth swing of the long, hooked blade, Silence began cutting a path through the tall grasses that grew on the mountainside. She worked with a steady rhythm and with the strength of trees as ancient as night. Sun had scarcely climbed to the navel of the sky when she reached the top of the mountain.

There she saw a large field where thick grasses grew like tears of an unseen sadness, and tall trees, like those which had raised her, stretched skyward.

Silence spoke to the trees, and they agreed to do what she asked. With great effort and much grunting, they pulled their roots from the ground and moved to the farthest edge of the field and there settled themselves back into the earth.

Now Silence could see the flat stones hidden among the grasses. With the scythe, she cut the grasses from around one stone and brushed the dirt from its face. The stone started to glow a pink as gentle and soft as a first kiss.

She laid the palm of a hand on the stone and whispered, "I came back. I came back." She felt the warmth of the stone's smile and wondered if it was her mother or father.

The next morning as she started up the mountain, the Iron Maker joined her, a scythe in his hands. Together the two worked quietly all that day, uncovering and cleaning more flat stones.

The next morning the Iron Maker brought his wife and daughters, while the Drum Maker came with his three sons, and the Basket Maker came with her four daughters. Soon the entire village was helping, and the field was quickly cleared. The flat stones shone hard like love that had been tested and prevailed.

Then Silence spoke. "I was sent back here to save Yesterday," she began, opening out her arms as if to embrace the flat stones that now seemed to be pulsing with life. "Here lie your parents and mine from Yesterdays so old you do not remember their names or their lives. They became angry because they did not like being forgotten. You cannot have Today without Yesterday. You may forget Yesterday, but it remembers you. Tonight we will remember all the Yesterdays with music, and dancing, and delicious food."

That afternoon the Drum Maker and his sons went through the village, their hands coaxing sounds of joy from the drums. With pots of food on their heads, the people followed the drummers up the mountain, dancing. Some took out cane fifes and gourd rattles, and when the people reached the top, they danced around the field and among the stones in a long line, holding each other's hands.

When Night told Sun to go to sleep, torches were lit. Lion opened his mouth and a roar so beautiful leaped from his throat that it turned into silver birds that took flight. Elephant raised her trunk and trumpeted a call that sounded like the stars were laughing, while Monkey sat high in a tree, gobbling food she had stolen from the villagers.

Then dark red lights rose from the flat stones like lost memories happy to have been found. The lights rippled languidly like slow-moving snakes, changing into yellows and blues and greens and oranges. They wove themselves around each other into braids, and then stretched out until they encircled the people of the village, holding them in an embrace as gentle as eternity.

Slowly the lights faded back into the stones, and there was only the night and stillness. Silence watched from the edge of the field, glad now that she had come back. Just as she started to wonder what she should do next, she felt herself being lifted gently onto the soft, broad-leafed branch of a tree. It was ThunderSnow. He carried her to another place where Yesterday longed for Today. And in the trees of the forest near the village, yellow pine needles became green, and old trees sang new songs.

When the people returned to the village, they realized that they had not seen Silence. They wanted to ask her to forgive them and to thank her for the blessing of Yesterday. But she knew, and from that time on, the people remembered.

AUTHOR'S NOTE

It was my fate as a child to be exposed to death on many occasions. I grew up in a slum neighborhood where children, teenagers, and adults I knew died in fires, automobile accidents, from stabbings, gunshots, and disease. I did not know then that in many cultures around the world people have shrines in their homes on which they place food for their dead, places where people visit cemeteries on one night of the year and eat meals at the graves of their loved ones and play music and dance. Throughout my life I have been drawn to walking through cemeteries, and even though I do not know anyone buried in them, it does not matter. It is important to remember the Ancestors, regardless of whose they are.

Someday each of us will be someone's ancestor, and we hope we are remembered. This story was written in honor of the Ancestors who have lived with and in me since I was born.

It is also written for all the children who know someone who has joined the Ancestors.